Zacharie & Jeremy
A supernatural encounter at the Louvre

Madelline R. Kennedy

ZACHARIE & JEREMY

A SUPERNATURAL ENCOUNTER AT THE LOUVRE

Based on a story by Jérôme Patalano

www.jeromepatalano.fr

Adaptation & Translation from French to US English: N.W. with DeepL
Cover: Natasha Snow Designs - www.natashasnowdesigns.com

Legal registration: October 2024
ISBN: 978-2-9589893-3-0
Story available in paperback and digital formats.

This queer book contains explicit content that may offend an uninformed reader.

This short story, originally in French, was first published under the title:

"Make your wishes"

in the anthology *Un homme pour Samhain*, out in November 2019 from Éditions Bookmark (Reines-Beaux collection).
Since withdrawn from sale, this story is offered here in an enriched version, and for the first time in English.

Chapter 1
Moving forward, despite everything

WhatsApp. From: Maxime.

Jeremy. I'm sorry in advance because I know this message will hurt you. I know you too well. But before anything else, I have to remind you that I really like you. With you by my side, I've been able to pull myself together these past few weeks and overcome my depression. Thank you for your support. But you should also know… I'm in the process of committing to someone else. He's like you, but the feelings… they can't be explained. I feel attracted to him. If

I'm better and more open now, it's thanks to you. In any case, I hope you won't mind...

A WhatsApp message with an aftertaste of romantic cruelty. Jeremy reread it intensely, over and over, his thumb scrolling across the screen as if waiting for a new one to appear. One, perhaps, that would say:

No, Jeremy! It's stupid what I'm doing. It's a mistake! I'm so fucking bad! What the hell did I send you? I shouldn't have! Will you forgive me?

Followed by:

Shall I come to your place tonight? I'll bring your favorite champagne and we'll talk about it together, all night if you like.

Accompanied by eggplant and droplet visual emojis.

But no, nothing else happened. Jeremy, a thirty-three-year-old curatorial apprentice at the prestigious Musée du Louvre, tall, boy-next-door, well-built, broad-shouldered and self-confident, didn't know what to say at the time. It was rare for someone to leave him speechless, but the sentimental uppercut was such that he'd been living for several days in a state of K.O. Should he have responded? The shock had been so immense.

This horrible missive, which tore at his insides every time he reread it and sometimes prevented him from breathing, was from Maxime, the young man he'd become infatuated with in recent months. Their involvement had begun when Maxime started messaging him one day on Instagram (he'd found him through mutual friends). Then from time to time, he'd message to talk about anything and everything, back when they'd bump into each other at the same fitness class, in the capital's most gay-friendly gym. Maxime knew he was handsome and played up to his good looks. No one was fooled by his false modesty when it was frequently made clear to him that he was an attractive boy. He was aware of the way men looked at him and suspected that many of them dreamed of counting him among their conquests, whether it be for life or for just a night. Wherever he showed his face, he was desired.

Jeremy would occasionally check him out at the gym, though he didn't dare make the first move. Being sociable, it was Maxime who ended up approaching Jeremy, much to the jealousy of many. For the young assistant at the Louvre, there was an instant click: one of the most attractive boys in the capital was interested in talking to him, and perhaps even more if Jeremy was so inclined. After a few inconsequential messages, they saw each other in real life, starting with coffees, then concerts, and then sex, which, unexpected as it was for Jeremy, was fireworks every time.

Maxime wasn't just handsome, he was charming, intelligent, cultured, and kept part of his life a secret. He was the kind of clean-cut, polite, well-dressed boy who appealed to mothers and grandmothers. This combination of things had captured Jeremy's heart unexpectedly, despite the warning from his new lover with the faux Apollo airs, who had been clear from the start of their relationship. He confessed that he didn't want to be "in a relationship," as he'd just come out of a complicated affair with an older man for whom he'd experienced strong feelings and which had ended badly. All he wanted was a friend with occasional sex. A sex friend, in short. But in spite of everything, Jeremy had begun to feel something that went beyond intimacy. He'd fallen in love with him, even though it wasn't mutual.

So, maybe feelings couldn't be explained in real

terms; but Jeremy didn't really believe in this idea, being so down-to-earth, with a rational answer to everything.

After the shock of reading the message, he had felt his legs go weak and had had to sit down quickly. He'd cried, too. A lot. Never had a message on WhatsApp inflicted such pain on him. It was like a stab wound. Maxime had let him dream, only to rip his heart out of his chest *(like the villain in Indiana Jones and the Temple of Doom)*, slice it open, spit in it, stomp on it with both feet and drive over it in a truck, before soaking it in gasoline and reducing it to ashes with the click of a lighter.

After the shock and tears, his indignation had risen sharply. Just a few days after receiving the message, Jeremy started to feel that he'd been treated unfairly, as sorrow gave way to anger. So, one of the capital's most prominent dandies was now living with someone? He'd soon changed his mind! Jeremy had been told what far too many people had heard before him: "I'm not looking for a relationship, I don't want that right now, I just got out of a complicated relationship." And now, this cad had allegedly found a 'guy like him' for whom he'd developed feelings. Seriously? A 'guy like him'?

What kind of phrase was that? He'd found Jeremy's twin and liked him better? If it hadn't been written with the sole purpose of hurting him, what else was it for?

So Jeremy counted for nothing? He was just a passing fancy? A free shrink who'd given alms with sex as payment?

The young assistant raged for days. How could Maxime have sent him such a message? Even if it were true, you shouldn't say it. He'd shown a terrible lack of tact; the mark of brilliant boys to whom society always forgives everything because they're a star. Jeremy wanted to scream, even to turn his apartment upside down in rage, but he didn't have the strength. So organized in his life and home, he was already tired at the mere thought of cleaning up what he would break.

❧

Slumped at his desk, in a tiny office where the sweet smell of dust mixed with incense, and mountains of books and other documents overloaded the too numerous shelves, Jeremy sighed as he reread the message.

Caroline, one of his closest friends and colleagues, stormed in with a cigarette in her mouth and files under her arms. Smoking was forbidden, but she didn't care. Her hard work and creative genius for staging exhibitions had turned the museum around in just a few years, and it was well worth closing your eyes (and your nose) to the fumes of ash upstairs.

In her early thirties, blonde, lanky, with piercing blue irises, she had a very trendy boho-chic look, unlike Jeremy, who sported a stricter shirt-tie-and-jacket style.

When she caught her colleague with his puppy-dog stare in front of his phone, she rolled her eyes and sighed:

"Are you still reading his messages? My word, you're going to make me depressed!" she complained, setting her files down with a clatter on her cluttered desk, while stubbing out her cigarette in an overloaded ashtray.

"I know..." he grumbled, without looking up.

It was too much, even for the force of nature that was Caroline. In a split second, she pounced on him and snatched his cell phone out of his hands.

"Hey, give it back!"

"No."

The "no" came out so brutally and with such a steady cold stare that Jeremy felt a chill. He knew Caroline, determined and ready for battle. He knew not to mess with her.

"I'm not giving it back to you until you make the effort to move on!" she blurted out.

"You're funny! I got dumped like a piece of shit and you want me to forget everything in two days?"

"Dumped? Dumped? You'd have had to be in a relationship to get dumped."

It was the one sentence that Jeremy absolutely didn't want to hear. Caroline, renowned for being outspoken, knew it would hit home. Seeing her best friend open his mouth and turn red with fury, she remained stoic and waited defiantly for his response. Finally, nothing came out. Jeremy calmed down and sank back into his chair, even more depressed. She lowered her voice and approached him.

"Jeremy, I understand what you're going through, believe me. It's hard. But you're going to have to learn to deal with it. I'll give you your cell phone back on the condition that you block his messages and stop dwelling on that damned conversation, okay?"

"Okay..." he sighed, without much conviction.

"I realize it's easier said than done, but frankly, let it go. Move on. This guy seemed nice on the surface, but he's made a fool of you, and that's the reality. He's not worth it."

"I know what you think of him..."

"Yeah, I hope so! Okay, he was handsome, cultured, intelligent, but he played with your feelings after clearly using you. He sucked all the energy out of you, only for him to get better and go elsewhere. You've got to get it through your head. He was a user. Plus... he was too young!"

Jeremy wrestled with this last point.

"Young, young... okay, he's nine years younger than me, but that doesn't mean anything."

"What it means is that at his age, he thinks he can do whatever he wants. These guys often get involved out of opportunism, and we've already talked about that. As luck would have it, he gets together with someone 'who looks like you.' I'll bet that the other guy has more money than you!"

"What does that mean?"

"Honestly, Jeremy, you're so naive. This guy has

hardly ever worked, hasn't finished law school, and is shacking up with more mature men with very good lifestyles. No, I'm telling you, I didn't have a good feeling about this guy from the start, and I was right! He was too good-looking and too clean-cut not to be hiding anything."

Jeremy couldn't get Maxime out of his head and fiddled with his phone before tucking it away in his pocket. Caroline, seeing him still brooding, tried a final motivational appeal.

"Besides, we've got bigger fish to fry than this buffoon! Let me remind you that we have THE event to finish for tomorrow, Halloween night. Sir Abernathy is stressed and if everything isn't in place for his party, we'll all be out of a job."

"Yeah, you're right," replied Jeremy, composing himself. "We've worked too hard on this exhibition and this party!"

"And with everything Iraq has lent us, we can't afford to mess it up. Are you coming? We've got to check out the gallery now."

❧

Jeremy jumped to his feet, motivated and

galvanized, and followed Caroline down the stairs to the Oriental Arts Department. Their mission was to assist their director, the exuberant English curator Sir James Abernathy and a well-informed Francophile.

Between the various museum offices, a fierce war waged in secret. Whoever had the most incredible idea that would draw the crowds would be favored internally. The venerable institution, although financially supported by the Ministry of Culture, had to constantly renew its offering to fill the coffers, as the many admissions (largely thanks to tourists) and store revenues were not enough.

In recent years, several themed exhibitions have gone viral around the world, Beyoncé and Jay-Z filmed a crazy music video there[1], AirBnB offered an exceptional night's sleep under the Louvre pyramid... All these events had helped the prestigious establishment to shine. But they were not to overshadow the very raison d'être of the museum: to showcase its permanent works, spread over square kilometers of galleries, as well

---

1 The Carters - Apeshit — and more recently Lady Gaga, who filmed a viral video for "Joker:Folie à deux".

as temporary collections and events, such as the recent Leonardo da Vinci retrospective in 2019. At the end of that year, a few months before lockdown, visitors had had to book their visit sometimes up to four months in advance! The Louvre loved that.

❧

Sir James Abernathy was both ecstatic and stressed with what he had brought back from Iraq, following years of bitter negotiations in this politically unstable country. Always dressed smartly, with silver curls and perfect poise, this British aristocrat was pacing up and down the main hall, where the gala evening 'Halloween: Oriental Myths and Masterpieces' was scheduled to take place. He watched anxiously as a dozen employees worked on the various relics, feeling useless and helpless in the face of time, which was passing far too quickly. Jeremy and Caroline found him among the many artifacts still being installed and approached him. They could feel his panic.

"Sir, are you all right?" asked Caroline.

"No, nothing is going right! Look at all this," he replied, feverish and on the verge of a nervous breakdown, waving his arms in all directions. "Things may be moving ahead for tomorrow's gala, but nothing's finished yet. I have a feeling this evening will be a complete failure!"

The curator was worried, and it showed in every pore. He was usually so calm and phlegmatic. Jeremy and Caroline had noticed the change in his behavior since his return from Iraq. Now he would panic at the drop of a hat, and his mood grew darker by the day. On the eve of the social event, he seemed to be at his wits' end, and the two young assistants put it down to stress.

"Sir, you can rely on our employees," tried Jeremy. "Everything is being installed by the specialized teams according to your requests. Look around you, everything will be ready in time for tomorrow night, rest assured!"

The curator spun around, and despite his wariness and arms occasionally swinging in the air to the rhythm of exaggerated exhalations, he could only see that his colleagues were right.

"It's true... I... I don't know what's gotten into me... It's enormous what's waiting for us here. There's so much pressure. Everything has to be perfect, you know? So much money has been invested, and profitability will pretty much depend on tomorrow night alone!"

"We know all about it," confirmed Caroline, touching his shoulder. "How about coming with us for a cup of tea and a breather?"

"Uh... Yeah... That's not a bad idea."

For Sir James Abernathy, a tea break was never a bad idea, whatever the time of day. Caroline and Jeremy knew their manager well enough to know that it was the ideal remedy for this mounting pressure. And so the three of them left the hustle and bustle, leaving the art directors to finish their work.

❧

As he too turned on his heels, Jeremy felt a chill and stopped dead in his tracks. Caroline and Sir Abernathy were moving away towards the elevators. It was as if a cool breeze had just caressed the back of his neck. The young man turned and scanned the room, looking for an open window. He turned around again and found himself facing one of the masterpieces of the forthcoming exhibition. An enormous clay amphora, over forty inches high and weighing more than four hundred and forty pounds, sealed by an unusual heavy bronze stopper, on which was engraved a terrifying face, that of a creature from the Abrahamic religions: the djinn.

It was the Varakk Vase.

He admired the relic, thousands of years old, as if hypnotized. He approached it, looking right and left, with the strange sensation of being spied upon. Except that nobody was paying any attention to him. He stepped forward, as if a connection had been established between himself and the amphora. Jeremy could no longer hear the hubbub around him and seemed to be under a spell. His eardrums were ringing. He felt as if he were alone in the world. His right hand reached up to touch the artifact, as if dominated by the irrepressible urge to caress it. A dark, distant whisper whistled in his ears. Intoxicated, his pulse and breathing quickened.

"Jeremy?"

Caroline had pounced on her colleague. The young man snapped out of his torpor, as if a fog had suddenly lifted. He heard again the din of the employees around him.

"What the hell were you doing? Are you nuts? Hands off! If Sir Abernathy had seen you, he'd have killed you, and not just metaphorically! Come on, we've got to help him lower his blood pressure or he'll be a nightmare tomorrow."

Jeremy looked confused. He hadn't had time to answer, disoriented, as if he'd been cut off. Plugged into automatic mode, his cheeks flushed with shame, he hurried after Caroline into the elevator where the curator was waiting, even more depressed than a few minutes before.

The young assistant forced himself to smile at his boss, and avoided Caroline's gaze. Something was troubling him, and he was struggling to come out of it. Had he gone into a trance? Why had he been drawn to this relic?

❧

It had been a long day for everyone. With just a few hours to go before the ceremony, everything had been set up and checked inside the Oriental Arts room, and the cleaning crew would take over to clean and polish overnight.

In this beautiful, immense square room, partly located in the basement, with its high concrete walls and glass ceiling, were displayed around a hundred different works, the vast majority on loan from Iraq. The country was open to culture and international exchanges, even if everyone knew it was still unstable, particularly since the withdrawal of American troops, which was decided almost overnight in December 2021, leaving a region bled dry after eighteen years of war.

There were oil lamps, wine bottles, sculptures of all sizes and strategically placed tableware. These artifacts, some dating back thousands of years, exuded a sense of grandiose history. The English curator had taken care to tell the story of Iraq, one of his favorite countries, over a period spanning several centuries, through these hundred or so exceptional objects. At the center of the room, the majestic Varakk Vase dominated the exhibition with its imposing stature.

Jeremy and Caroline had spent the rest of the day securing the arrival of the guests of honor for the gala, before finally returning home at nightfall. They had left Sir Abernathy alone in his office, still wrapping things up with just a few hours to go before the evening of October 31st, which was now fast approaching.

Leaving his office around midnight, the director

diverted his attention to the retrospective he was about to reveal to the world. There, he came across the cleaners, chasing away every last ounce of dust, which in this centuries-old place, was a challenge. He smiled politely at the employees, who packed up their belongings and left.

Now alone in this large, half-lit room, Sir Abernathy enjoyed his exhibition, the one he'd been designing for years. The place was softly lit by the small lamps on the shelves laden with works of art, and by the full moon shining through the glass vault, lending an almost mystical aura to the retrospective. Sir Abernathy couldn't help but inspect the installations one by one with his finger, checking one last time that everything had been placed according to the plans he had drawn up. In this quiet place, only his heels echoed with every step on the sandstone floor.

Having fallen in love with the cultures of Iraq at a young age, he had always wanted to pay tribute to this country battered by decades of dictatorship and war. The objects on display here had all been chosen, researched and negotiated for. They all told a glorious story of the past.

His gaze caught the imposing centerpiece of

the gallery, the djinn vase. Sir Abernathy had often felt drawn to this gigantic object, especially since he had brought it back in person, aboard a special boat chartered by the French navy.

Chapter 2
The encounter

Two months earlier.

"Are you sure you don't want to join us on deck?" shouted the captain to make himself heard.

The noise of the machinery, combined with that of the huge waves outside, echoed deafeningly in the ship's hold. The storm was raging and the sea was rough.

"No, I'm fine, thanks! I have to inspect everything we're bringing back to Paris one more time," exclaimed Sir Abernathy, always neat and tidy despite nature's rampage.

"All right, I'll leave you to it. But don't stay here too long, you might get sick or fall! I want to see you up there with us in ten minutes, okay?"

"I promise!"

The captain climbed back up onto the deck with difficulty, using the stairs to cling to the handrails and resist the rolling motion. Between the waves that violently battered the boat's hull, the violence of the ocean and the worrying screeching of steel, the noises gave the impression that their little freighter would soon be torn apart.

He left Sir Abernathy in the middle of the Dantesque crates, which had been stacked with care to avoid irreversible damage during the crossing to France. So far, nothing had fallen. Faced with this mountain of packages, the curator hoped the whole thing would hold together until the weather calmed down.

Of all the artifacts laid and held in place within this mound of treasures from the Orient, only one hadn't been able to be packed, officially due to its size and weight. Anchored on all sides, the djinn vase sat "naked" at the bottom of the hold, between all the other boxes.

The pretext of weight and size was quickly found by Sir Abernathy to justify this unprotected import to the captain, who was worried about insurance policies. In reality, due to strong local beliefs, the curator had been unable to call on anyone in Iraq to make a custom wooden crate. He had always found the doors closed, especially those of local carpenters, who had been terrified by Varakk's amphora and had all refused to work on it. "I don't want to stir up the devil's wrath," he had often heard. Sir Abernathy had therefore decided, with the help of less superstitious Iraqi colleagues, to strap the impressive vase to the boat with strong cables to prevent any accidental damage to the artifact. The operation, perilous and fraught with responsibility, took several hours.

❧

Sir Abernathy, trying to keep his balance, consulted his masterpiece and approached it, proudly. He had been working for years with the Iraqi authorities on this exceptional exhibition! And the result, around a hundred objects, was well worth the effort. The whole of Paris would be talking about this collection, there was no doubt. Few retrospectives in the City of Light had created such a stir for a long time; a dozen, at most, over the last two decades. His would be a success!

He had been able to negotiate most of the artifacts without any problems, even if the exchanges had lasted several years. After all, haggling over "loans" from regional museums, or even wealthy individuals, was never easy in the closed world of art. But in the end, he had succeeded.

Until one day, in his quest for rare items, he stumbled upon something he'd never seen before. Hidden in the cellar of an unscrupulous wealthy ambassador, the Varakk Vase lay hidden from view. When he was invited to the owner's home by a local curator, Sir Abernathy was stunned by the amphora's Dantesque dimensions. He had never seen one so large! The engraving of the djinn's face on the bronze stopper and on one side of the vase reminded him of Medusa, one of the snake-haired Gorgons of Greek mythology. According to legend, those who met her gaze when her head was uncovered were immediately petrified.

Something had immediately appealed to Sir Abernathy when he saw the vase. He wasted no time in requesting authentication. The results of the study, which came in a few weeks later, proved that it was indeed a piece dating back hundreds of years

BC, but this carbon-14 validation didn't explain Sir Abernathy's relentless diplomatic drive to repatriate it to Paris. It was what it evoked in the locals when Sir Abernathy talked about it.

He had seen the reaction of most of them. One even shouted at him, "Never take that amphora! Or evil will befall you! Never!" Such deep-rooted superstition made him wonder. Why were the locals so afraid of it? Were they right? Until one day, he discovered a very old legend.

According to local mythology, this enormous amphora was the central figure in a past mythological war, in which 'magical creatures' took part in a decisive battle alongside humans. Sir Abernathy smiled, for he loved folklore, without necessarily believing it.

Varakk, the djinn whose head was engraved on the side of the vase and on its heavy bronze stopper, is said to have been invoked by an ancient king wishing to acquire power and eternal life. Also called "Efrit", or evil genie, the spirit, whose true appearance was unknown, is said to have listened to the king's requests and granted his wishes. But the sovereign was fooled. For the first few days, his wishes had certainly come true. He had felt invigorated, as if possessed by a second youth. He had been endowed with incredible physical strength. Galvanized, he launched his armies against neighboring countries to rule them. This had lasted a few months, during which he had been victorious.

But his wishes soon backfired. In reality, this evil genie deceived the king by dangling dreams of glory in front of his eyes, and, without warning, set a date for his demise. One wartime setback followed another, his vitality faded and his physical strength left him. One day, exhausted and on the ground, sickly and weak and on the verge of being deposed, he faced Varakk, who once again presented himself to him. Looking down on this pleading king, crawling on the ground and kissing his feet, the evil spirit suppressed him and taught him that making wishes was actually dangerous, because requests, often greedy, sent you straight to hell. And so, the monarch incurred the wrath of the demon, who sent him to one of the many hells in existence, the one reserved for the greedy, to undergo an eternity of suffering.

Varakk was indeed one of the few evil djinn who served Evil. He wanted only one thing each time he was called upon: to emerge from his prison of clay and bronze to summon the Darkness to invade planet Earth.

With the king out of the way, Varakk opened a passageway to a terrifying Otherworld. And in the process, he summoned the monsters of the underworld to eliminate the mortals and pave the way for his supreme master to take their place. Immense clouds would cover all the countries of the globe at once, immersing the Earth in darkness overnight. The end of civilization as it then existed approached.

Except that Varakk's awakening would provoke another: Bolaam. Yin can't live without Yang...

Legend has it that another genie, Bolaam, stepped in to counter Varakk as he began to plunge humans into the chaos of darkness. Riding on the back of Bahamut, a mythological dragon of Dantesque size and immemorial strength, the fabulous warrior fought alongside powerful supernatural creatures whose sole mission was to protect the Earth, and who he summoned with a magical ancestral talisman.

At the end of an epic battle, Bolaam is said to have succeeded in trapping Varakk in his vase carved in the depths of the underworld, sealing the bronze plug that closed it and putting an end to the conflict.

A story worthy of 'The Thousand and One Nights' tales that had enchanted Sir Abernathy upon reading them. He needed this amphora at all costs! In the storytelling he intended to develop for his exhibition, he had felt from the start that something was missing. Now he had it. Varakk, a magical tale, a legend that he would proudly tell in Paris to impress the gallery, especially during the retrospective's publicity campaigns. A story like that was bound to attract the crowds and bring in money for the Louvre's coffers, on a par with the Egyptian exhibition events that had always been popular in the capital.

❧

As Sir Abernathy silently admired his amphoraI in the hold of the boat, which was still swaying as hard as ever, a powerful wave slammed against the hull. The curator lost his balance and, almost falling, leaned on the gigantic vase, which had not slipped one iota thanks to the straps. But the heavy bronze cork had moved by a few inches. A small empty space between the container and the outside had formed without him realizing it.

The djinn's engraved eyes suddenly shone with a brilliant light. Rising to his feet, Sir Abernathy found himself trapped in its field of vision. A mad energy invaded him and his body went numb. Faced with the increasingly radiant face, the curator was electrified. He tried to open his mouth to speak, but no sound came out. His eyes turned white. Trance-like and hypnotized, none of his limbs moved. It was as if he'd just looked at Medusa and was about to turn into a stone statue. Barely conscious, he heard dark, guttural, ancestral, grumbling whispers insidiously penetrating his mind. His mouth twitched with an ancient dialect while he was still leaning against the vase, as if possessed.

It was no longer him in the hold. It was someone else.

"Sir, are you all right?" called the captain, worried. "Did something break? My crew saw the light coming from below!"

The glow emanating from the djinn's face suddenly faded. The curator's possession came to a screeching halt. His eyes widened, returning to normal. Still leaning against the vase, he withdrew his hand, afraid of damaging the artifact. Groggy, dry-mouthed, he couldn't regain his composure. What had just happened? Had he suffered a blackout?

From the top of the stairs, the captain could see nothing. But hearing no response from Abernathy, he descended in fourth gear, fearing that the curator had fallen, or worse. He came face to face with the Louvre professional, who was pale and staggering, as if his legs could no longer carry him.

"I... I... Well, yes, I think so," replied Sir Abernathy.

The captain was well aware that the man in charge of the Louvre seemed lost. Nausea from heavy swells, perhaps. It could happen to anyone, even the most adventurous.

"As we were pitching hard just now, I was worried about you," replied the commander. "Come with us up there. You must travel with the others on the deck. Your safety is at stake. As captain, I have to use my authority to oblige you to follow me. Please do so now."

The still bewildered curator nodded like a scolded child and sheepishly went with the captain, leaving only his precious artifacts in the hold.

From now on, they were no longer alone...

Chapter 3
Wake-up calls

Alone, in the dim half-light of the museum, when it was already dark outside, Sir Abernathy admired the Varakk Vase. Only a few hours to go before he revealed his retrospective to the world, and this majestic amphora was sure to impress the public!

Unbeknown to the curator, the atmosphere in the showroom gradually became heavy and electric. The natural light of the moon faded. The few small lanterns lit on the shelves dimmed. The place was veiled in darkness.

Suddenly, the eyes of the face engraved on the vase, that of the djinn, glowed intensely, startling Sir Abernathy. He barely had time to react when a powerful white beam burst from the genie's mouth and struck him on the forehead.

An abrupt force held him back, paralyzing and shackling him. Something entered him, leaving him no choice, piercing the darkness of the gallery. Sir Abernathy, standing stiffly, screamed in terror; he couldn't stop the force from seeping into his head.

Then, the intense milky light disappeared quickly, plunging the Louvre room back into darkness. You could have heard a pin drop. The eyes of the engraved djinn stopped glowing, but remained incandescent.

Sir Abernathy pulled himself together.

But he wasn't himself anymore.

His pupils had turned scarlet, his face was placid, and a slight sneer played at the corner of his lips. He knelt in front of the vase. The demonic spirit that possessed him spoke to him in his mind.

"Oh inferior race, pledge allegiance to me!"

"I'm all yours, Master."

"Help me out of this jail! I've been locked up here too long! It's time for my revenge! You know what I need most to regain my strength, don't you?"

"Yes. You need human wishes..."

"That's right! I want wishes! Find me some

envious earthlings who will contribute to my rebirth!"

"Master, tomorrow is the most prestigious of evenings. There will be a lot of people there before the official inauguration. I'll ask them to make wishes for you..."

"Good! And I'll make them come true for them! I need as many wishes as possible to help me get out of this prison. Greedy, avaricious wishes... And thus open the mouth of the Other World. An army awaits its revenge and is impatient. I'm counting on you!"

"Rest assured, Master, you'll get what you ask for. Tomorrow evening, the Earth will make your acquaintance, and it will be grandiose!"

The djinn's voice fell silent and his hold on Sir Abernathy was lifted. The engraving's eyes faded and the obscure veil that had plunged the room into darkness dissipated. The faint light of the moon illuminated the gallery, as did the small lights.

Slowly, the curator came to his senses. Lost and dry-mouthed, he couldn't understand why he'd dropped to one knee. He straightened up, embarrassed, with no further memory, and thought he must have blacked out for a moment. This worried him at the time, as he could be a bit of a hypochondriac. He looked around the room to see if anyone had seen him, ran his hands over his shirt and nervously rubbed his suit jacket. Still confused, he swiveled around, trying to remember, but nothing came back to him. Fatigue must have been the reason for his blackout, he convinced himself.

He looked at his watch, which read 3:30am, and was startled. He'd been here for over an hour! Worried that he wouldn't be prepared for the day ahead, he decided to head home as quickly as possible, but not without a final inspection of the relics installed next to the Vase of Varaks. Tomorrow is another day, he thought. Once the gala evening was over, he'd have plenty of time to catch his breath. Now was not the time to let off steam.

As he left the room after turning off the last lights, he didn't realize that various artifacts and objets d'art throughout the Louvre had also begun to glow.

❧

In the vast Haussmannian apartment above Zacharie, the chic former boutique of a renowned antique dealer, not far from the Louvre and overlooking the Tuileries gardens, something was sparkling.

An old amulet glowed, set among a jumble of shelves filled with documents and archaeological artifacts of all kinds. The unobtrusive light grew brighter and brighter, quickly illuminating the office like daylight. A man in his late thirties, tall, muscular and broad-shouldered, dressed only in boxer shorts with his eyes still numb from sleep, scrambled up and pounced on the talisman that continued to sparkle in his hands.

He analyzed the object and caressed it gently. He studied it feverishly from every angle before placing it in a box he'd unearthed from one of his many drawers in order to hide the glimmering light. Then he smiled.

"At last," he murmured. "I've wanted this mission for so long!"

He couldn't wait to hear about the legend he'd been waiting for... for centuries.

Chapter 4
The Big Night

The gala evening had finally arrived. The long line of guests stretched for a hundred meters outside on the Rue de Rivoli, crowding the sidewalks already overloaded by the City of Paris's eternal construction work. The many hand-picked guests were congregating in the autumn chill, glittering in chic outfits to honor the event. There was electricity in the air as impatient guests waited to go in and VIPs, who were dropped off in cabs, headed straight to the front of the line. Freeloaders also tried to get in, only to be turned away by Caroline and Jeremy, luxury hosts dressed to the nines. A classic event in the City of Lights.

Everyone was there, and the evening seemed set for success. Once inside, the privileged guests invited to this unusual event gravitated to the relics, cocktail or champagne in hand. Some recognized and greeted each other while some stayed with their friends. Others chatted at length, eager to catch up. But everyone came with the same curiosity: the exhibition itself. The imported pieces were channeled by a well-thought-out path of light. The story told by Sir Abernathy, followed to the letter by everyone thanks to the obligatory marked route, remained both simple to understand and addictive. Everyone agreed that the retrospective was grandiose, as was the evening, which was organized to perfection and lived up to all expectations. Journalists and photographers, also present and hand-picked, were there not just to film a red carpet, but to ensure that as many articles as possible were written to provide the expected media coverage.

For his part, the curator, who had initially received the event's main sponsors, floated from guest to guest to show off, but above all to ensure that the launch of his exhibition remained under control. Jeremy and Caroline watched over the entrance and greeted those on the guest list, then sometimes took on the roles of barmaid and waiter as they were called upon to lend a hand. They weren't proud; when you were just an assistant, you had to be motivated if you wanted to secure your place at the Louvre. The evening was so exciting that they stifled the fatigue of the last few months.

•

By 11pm, the room was packed and exuded a deliciously chic ambience. Time for the two assistants to take a well-deserved break, champagne glass in hand. Not far from the djinn vase, Jeremy and Caroline glanced discreetly at the guests.

"There are some hot guys here tonight," remarked Caroline, with a touch of greed on her lips.

"Yeah, maybe," grumbled Jeremy, sounding blasé.

"Since when do you play hard to get?"

"I don't mean to be picky, but let's just say my head's not in it and..."

"Oh fuck! Don't turn around! Don't you dare!"

Too late, curiosity had quickly taken over. Jeremy swiveled and saw Maxime approaching, triumphant, in a beautiful suit that fitted him perfectly. Maxime. Champagne in hand, his presence radiated around the room, carried by a sparkling smile.

The young assistant watched him walk towards him, his throat dry and his breathing instantly halted. Both hypnotized and frightened to discover him here after his last message a few days ago, Jeremy could no longer think clearly. He was frozen. He had the impression that his ex-lover was walking towards him in slow motion, like in a Netflix teen soap opera. Until a man in his early thirties stopped Maxime in his tracks. Jeremy saw this as an opportunity to leave the scene, but could think of nothing better than to turn around in a panic to face a distressed Caroline.

"What the hell's he doing here?" asked a frightened Jeremy.

"I don't fucking know!" replied Caroline. "We didn't invite him, though. Wait... Did we?"

She racked her brains, confused.

"Ah!" she continued. "He must have come with one of our contacts who received entry tickets, with an authorized plus-one!"

She looked over her friend's shoulder, who didn't know what to do with himself, his anxiety having raised another notch.

"They seem very close, the two of them..." she commented.

"Is that him? You think he's the guy who...?"

"Who looks like you? I hope not!" she snapped. "He's nothing like you! You're better looking. He reeks of money, I swear it. That's what must have attracted Maxime. That gold-digger!"

"How do you know?"

"A woman knows these things," she admitted, continuing to spy on the two men in the distance.

"Trust me on that. No, I'm telling you. He's not that charming. He doesn't deserve you! Well, if he does..."

"What am I doing? I don't feel well right now..."

Jeremy was sinking in panic.

"Oh, shit!" said Caroline.

"What?"

"Put on your best smile and..."

"Hi Jeremy!" said Maxime.

The young assistant, with his back to Maxime, closed his eyes and tried to pull himself together. He had to turn around, but his body wouldn't let him. He took a deep breath, forcing himself, before turning and trying to show off his best 'perfect evening' self. Faced with Maxime, even more charming up close, his heart almost exploded.

"Hi Caroline," Maxime continued, addressing her with a polite smile.

"Bonsoir Maxime," she replied curtly with a murderous look.

Everyone knew that when Caroline greeted someone by clearly stating their first name, it was either to be solemn or to express an underlying reproach. In this case, it was the latter. The ex-lover pretended he hadn't understood the nuance and addressed Jeremy again, who, paralyzed, still hadn't uttered a single word.

"When André suggested this evening," Maxime continued, "I didn't hesitate for a second. You've told me so much about this fabulous project over the last few months that I had to see it for myself!"

On the surface, he seemed happy for Jeremy. Jeremy was dismayed.

"An... André?" stammered the assistant.

The man "in his early thirties" he'd seen approaching Maxime a few seconds earlier also approached, cocktail in hand. Tall, dark-haired, with an elaborate three-day beard, an open-necked shirt and a slightly baggy jacket, Jeremy found him rather handsome, but nothing more. There were thousands of others like him. Next to him, Maxime, in his tailored Italian suit and perfectly styled, spiky hair, shone with far more charm in his eyes.

"Pleased to meet you, André," replied Jeremy politely, shaking his hand.

An icy chill seemed to have settled between the four of them. Caroline glared at Maxime. Maxime's companion was sipping his drink, a good excuse for remaining silent.

"Jeremy, Caroline!" hailed Sir Abernathy, not far away. "I need your help!"

Saved by the bell, thought his assistants. Just in time.

"Sorry, work, we've got to go," Caroline said without a second thought. With a slightly haughty expression, she grabbed her petrified colleague.

"Jeremy?" said Maxime.

"Yes?" he replied as Caroline dragged him away.

"Can we still talk?"

"I... yes..." he murmured, striding away without another word.

They rejoined their curator.

"You called us, Sir Abernathy?" asked Caroline as Jeremy straightened his suit.

"My friends! Are you ready? It won't be long before we start making our wishes. You'll keep a close eye on everything, won't you? Five minutes!"

"Sir Abernathy, you can count on us!" replied a proud Caroline.

Their manager, clearly pleased with the way the evening was going, stepped aside, leaving them alone again. Jeremy turned around, discreetly this time, to see Maxime having a great time with the *rich-looking-thirty-something-who-was-like-him*. Given their gestures, laughter and closeness, there was no doubt that it was this stranger who had replaced him.

Jeremy couldn't help thinking back to their last months together. They say that when someone is about to die, their life flashes before their eyes. But no one talks about the 'malaise of the ex.' Because the same thing happens to everyone who still cares deeply about their ex: they too see this kind of image flash before their eyes every time they come across their lost love.

A flood of memories resurfaced. Their first

meetings. Staring at each other at the gym. Saying hello to each other in the same classes. Then, their first exchanges, in the hallway, recovering from the class they'd just taken. All sweaty. Soaked-through T-shirts clinging to their bodies. Jeremy remembered devouring him with his eyes on several occasions, all the while remaining discreet. When Maxime didn't show up for class, which was rare, he felt a twinge of sadness. Because if you're going to suffer at the gym, you might as well do it while looking at something good.

In purely physical terms, Maxime was finely muscled. A man's body like any other, well proportioned, not too bulky or thin. A flat stomach and broad, yet discreet shoulders. The kind of chest that gives you a nice surprise when he takes off his shirt. And his thighs? What thighs! Jeremy's favorite part of a man's body. They looked powerful, as did his shapely calves. Maxime knew that his physique was an eye-catcher and a source of fantasy. In addition to his handsome face and endearing smile, his dressed-up look of a 19th century romantic hero, which he maintained through a meticulous wardrobe, was a real turn-on. He must have been the reincarnation of a male fictional hero, *Lady*

Chatterley's lover or Julien Sorel from Stendhal's *Le Rouge et le Noir*.

In civilian life, he looked like a university professor, which he actually was at times, because on the side, he was struggling to finish his law thesis and lacked the money to live on. The kind of young teacher many people fantasized about, and from whom they wanted only one thing: for him to invite them into his office, out of sight, for something controlled and consensual.

In bed? Maxime hid his game well. Pure on the outside, he looked like butter wouldn't melt, but he was a different person when it came to very private situations. Jeremy had even been surprised by this at first, as he was no stranger to exploring the limits of his own sexuality. On the few occasions they'd slept together, it had been... wild. Maxime was the enterprising type, but liked the other to take things firmly in hand.

In Jeremy's apartment, they'd used every room and their bodies had reacted in perfect harmony. Roles didn't need to be defined. It was fluid and in sync. Sometimes it was cute or cuddly, and other times it was wilder and more adventurous. Sometimes it involved sex toys to spice things up.

Other times, one wore a daring special outfit that the other looked at greedily. Their body-to-body encounters ended up feverish, sweaty and sticky with passion, often requiring a change of sheets. They knew every inch of each other. Jeremy had a particular attraction to Maxime's firm buttocks. Maxime, on the other hand, loved to explore Jeremy with his tongue, everywhere. Everywhere. And he was good at it. Despite his young age, his technique was perfect, honed by experience that Jeremy guessed was already long and rich. Their desire had often been expressed as if it would be the last time they'd ever touch each other. The intensity was insane and memorable. The upstairs neighbors had even banged on their ceiling because they'd cried out too loud in the night. And they laughed about it, embarrassed at the time... but not too much.

Then, one day, things suddenly slowed down. Although still not officially a couple, they saw each other less. Until Jeremy received the famous, murderous message on WhatsApp, which plunged him into total confusion.

❧

"No, but who does he think he is?" stormed Caroline.

"Well, it's Sir Abernathy, he has the right to..."

"I'm not talking about Sir Abernathy! I'm talking about Maxime! I'm furious! He's come to hurt you, I'm sure of it!"

Caroline wouldn't give up. She felt sorry for her friend, who she saw was suffering.

""Oh dear." She calmed down. "Do you want me to get rid of him?"

"Huh?"

"I can!" she continued, smiling sadistically. "I don't know how, but I can kick him and his sugar daddy out in no time! And I'd love to!"

"But..."

"Or do you want me to beat him up? I can pay some guys to beat him up, if that would make you happy..."

"Huh? You're not serious, are you?"

"No, of course not. I'm kidding," she said coldly, sipping what was left of her champagne.

Jeremy didn't know if she was joking and almost shuddered.

"So Jeremy," she continued, determined. "Take action now. What you need is a rebound guy!"

"A what?"

"A rebound guy! We all need one, especially after a break-up. Basically, a man you're not necessarily going to get attached to, but who's going to help you forget your ex, thanks to a wild romp between consenting adults."

"You think so?"

"You bet! Find yourself someone who you'll have a great time with sexually, knowing that there'll be nothing more between you."

She took another sip of champagne as she scanned the room until her eyes caught sight of a potential target.

"Look at that guy over there!" she said, pointing to a handsome young man toward the back of the room. "He's been staring at you all evening."

With short, light-brown hair, a slender body enhanced by his perfectly-fitting suit, and sublime green eyes, he was very elegant and seductive. A model, probably of Iberian origin, like those in certain sexy Spanish TV series. He was casting insistent glances at Jeremy, who admired him from head to toe, before turning back to Caroline, looking blasé.

"Let it go, Caro. He's the archetypal rich kid who

knows he's hot, but wants us to believe he doesn't know it. Who thinks he's entitled to everything because he's part of the 'beautiful' crowd. Who must have an Insta feed overflowing with sublime shots of himself produced by excellent 'amateur' photographers..." he mimed the quotation marks, "... who were really only hoping for one thing: to sleep with him. Especially when they asked him to pose shirtless or in Rodin's thinker-style boxer shorts from the 21st century in front of a poor Haussmann facade, somewhere in Montmartre. But of course, it was never going to happen, because he 'values their friendship,' you know. As a result, they got screwed, so to speak, while he got free star portraits to reassure his 'real self', who's so shy and doesn't really want to talk about himself. Although, in reality, that's all he does. He posts bullshit about self-esteem and the importance of being in the moment while in truth, he doesn't understand a word of it and only got an F in philosophy at high school. He's also the king of selfies and Insta stories to show off his awesome life. But in reality, he's a chronic depressive who's only interested in collecting likes because he doesn't have any real friends or loving relatives in his inner circle."

If she'd been a manga character, Caroline would have found herself with big, bewildered eyes, a mouth hanging open in surprise and a large drop running down the side of her head.

"Jesus! You figured all that out in just two seconds?"

"A custom of the Parisian queer scene..." her colleague sighed, already tired of it. "These guys are a horror. And they're all switching over to TikTok right now to make empty 'moi, moi' lives, or worse, making videos telling us what they do all day, from the moment they wake up to the moment they go to bed, and conveniently, 90% of the time, topless."

"You'll have to give me their accounts then," Caroline responded, licking her lips and pulling out her smartphone to open the app. "I'm very curious, you know."

But Jeremy didn't look up, serious.

"No, believe me, these guys are a no-go," he confirmed.

"Wait, we're not asking you to put a ring on his finger either and then officially become his TikTok camera guy. Just go and have fun with him! Feel another body on you for just one night – that's a rebound guy! Afraid he'll get attached? Don't let him. Take control! Enjoy the guys and get your revenge."

The Spanish model turned around once more and stared at Jeremy in an ever more insistent way that spoke volumes.

""Look how he's devouring you with his eyes..." Caroline began again, "...almost hungrily. Do you want me to check for you that he's gay?"

"How?"

"I downloaded Grindr on my mobile."

"You? Since when?"

"I installed it to stalk guys when I'm just flirting. You know, these days, us straight cis women aren't always too sure about people's orientation... So, rather than waste my time, I thought of this! And I'm not the only one, believe me. For your sake, I hope he's gay, because if he isn't, I'd fuck him!"

Jeremy was so taken aback by this revelation that he decided not to raise his voice, and downed what champagne he had left.

Chapter 5
Make your wishes

A certain frenzy began in the room around them. At Sir Abernathy's request, guests were hurrying to line up in front of the exhibition's grandiose amphora to respond, amused, to the game the curator had devised by way of entertainment.

"Come closer, come closer!" he invited them. "It's time to see if the legends are true! Line up in front of the Vase of Varakk and make your wish. And who knows? Maybe it'll come true!"

The guests smiled along with Sir Abernathy, and applauded.

A few weeks earlier, when Jeremy and Caroline were looking for concepts to animate the gala, they found Sir Abernathy's idea rather original. Asking their evening guests to play on the ancestral codes of wishing upon djinns, so famous in fairy tales and legends, to get them to admire the vase, was a good idea. And it was clear that, on this inaugural evening, the guests were happy to get involved.

The two assistants heard everything from the more predictable requests ("I want to be rich and famous") to the whimsical ones ("I want my boss to fall in love with me") to the most serious desires ("I wish I'd given more of myself to my parents before they died"). People were having fun because they were a bit tipsy and they thought the game was harmless fun.

Except no one realized that, with every wish they made, Varakk was building up a monster's worth of energetic power. The engraving of his face on the vase seemed to be gradually changing color, and even... to be displaying a slight demonic smile.

❧

Antique dealer Zacharie, his broad shoulders encased in a suit far too tight for his build, watched the circus of wishes from a distance, sipping his glass of champagne. He approached the vase cautiously and listened to the wishes as he analyzed the artifact. The way he moved was almost feline. He seemed fascinated by the thousand-year-old piece, which he wanted to touch with his fingertips.

Very handsome with blue eyes and a physique that was evident through his too-tight clothes, he had the head of an American football player, with perfect features and a square jaw. His tall stature and presence hadn't escaped Jeremy's notice. Jeremy took pleasure in checking him out as he started another glass of champagne. Meanwhile, Caroline continued to extol the intrinsic bodily qualities of the model she thought Jeremy should spend a night with to forget Maxime. But he wasn't listening.

For Jeremy, if there was one man he could consider a rebound guy tonight, it was this anonymous, dark-haired, blue-eyed man who seemed fascinated by the Varakk Vase. Someone seemingly older, no doubt with experience, capable of gripping him firmly and confidently for a few torrid hours. Or so he thought, because he didn't know. Was he even gay? But the very sight of him aroused Jeremy. Excitement stirred in his crotch and tickled his insides.

Caroline was right, after all. Maxime had probably gone to the party to hurt him, and his manipulative feelings had blown up in his face. Jeremy decided to go for it. He was going to have fun tonight. And this stranger could help. But how to approach him? Did he like men? One of the eternal questions that comes up when you're gay... The stranger wasn't looking at him, as he remained captivated by the long line of guests stretching out to make wishes.

Suddenly, the young assistant had an idea.

"Caro, follow me!"

He took her by the hand and shamelessly cut the line of guests. A little tipsy, they both stood in front of the Vase of Varakk to submit a wish, while apologizing to those who were waiting, explaining that they were the organizers of the event. A splendid justification, since the guests didn't hold it against them and thanked them for a successful evening.

Zacharie, the handsome thirty-something Jeremy had been fantasizing about for a few minutes, came closer to them and listened, curious. Both surprised and frightened, he watched the amphora, then Jeremy. The assistant finally met his gaze. As they made eye contact, the young man's body was electrified. He smiled, and suddenly endowed with a strength he didn't know he had, launched into his request:

"Djinn Varakk. I vow to be self-confident. To approach who I want, when I want, to seduce without consequence, without pain, and to no longer suffer because of my feelings."

Calm settled in. And a few seconds felt like a long time. Caroline squeaked between sips. Nothing happened.

"It's a rotten wish," she said to break the silence. "Do what everyone else does. Ask to be Jeff Bezos, a rock star or own a harem of boys, I don't know..."

"It just came to me. I'm tired of suffering in love. That's what I want. Guys, with a snap of my fingers. You want me to have fun without consequences? I said it to Varakk! What if it comes true? We'll find out!"

He chuckled to himself and left the queue with Caroline, leaving the guests to express their wishes. As he left, he caught the handsome stranger smiling at his wish and looking at him one last time. Did it mean anything?

Further into the room, out of breath and laughing heartily, they realized they'd been part of the folklore they themselves found hard to believe. Suddenly, Nathalie, another assistant from the Louvre, pounced on them, looking serious and stressed.

"Have you seen Sir Abernathy?"

"Uh... no," stammered Caroline, sheepishly.

"We ran into him about ten minutes ago," Jeremy conceded, a little embarrassed to be enjoying the evening while their curator was in demand.

Dejected, their colleague rolled her eyes and walked away, splitting the crowd. Jeremy and Caroline looked at each other, feeling foolish.

"You think that..." Caroline hesitated.

"Yes!" cut in Jeremy. "Our break's over. Let's go and get him!"

Spinning around in a hurry, Jeremy bumped into antique dealer Zacharie, who had moved in behind him, without him realizing it. In the process, the entirety of his champagne flute spilled onto his guest's white shirt with a resounding splash, soaking it in alcohol. The young man was paralyzed with embarrassment and his guest's face was frozen in surprise. Caroline, always a step ahead, had already moved away, leaving her colleague alone.

"Oh sorry! Sorry! Sorry! I'm so sorry!"

He placed his empty glass on the tray of a passing waiter and pulled a tissue from his pocket to dab up the mess.

"Come on, it's not serious," replied the handsome man. "It's not your fault. You didn't see me and I should have been more careful."

"Maybe, but as one of the evening's organizers, I feel like an idiot. I have to fix this. I'm so sorry!"

"Don't worry, I'll to the bathroom downstairs to dry off."

"Then I'll come with you!"

The handsome thirty-something smiled.

"There's no need, I can do it myself, you know..."

"I insist! I'll come with you," said Jeremy, red-faced with embarrassment.

Without another second's thought, the two of them headed for the stairs leading to the basement. As they passed, Zacharie glanced at the line of people making wishes, which had grown longer, and looked annoyed.

In the distance, the young Spanish model saw them leave together.

In the unoccupied, sanitized basement toilet, Jeremy pounced on the tissue dispenser. He took far too many in one go and then rushed back to the attractive man whose name he still didn't know, to mop up the spilt champagne.

"No, really, don't worry," insisted the man, embarrassed.

"Yes, yes, I have to do something. You're a guest and I don't want to spoil the evening we've worked so hard to organize."

Zacharie didn't flinch, seeing Jeremy busily at work on the stain and realizing that he wasn't about to let go anytime soon. For greater ease, the antique dealer removed his jacket. His shirt, slim-fitting, left little to the imagination. The champagne had made the garment translucent, and it now clung to his flat, toned stomach.

"Pull your shirt out! We'll dry it faster with the hand drier," said Jeremy, more decisive this time.

Zacharie replied with a smile and the two locked eyes. Jeremy's pupils turned scarlet and his guest found himself instantly in his host's grip.

"Do as I ask," the assistant urged, more authoritatively.

In the exhibition hall, the eyes on Varakk's

face grew brighter and brighter. Another wish was coming true.

The thirty-something who Jeremy had furtively fantasized about earlier said nothing. It was as if he'd been petrified and his brain was taking note of the command. His gaze changed. Something had taken possession of him. His eyes fixed on Jeremy's, and he answered calmly, like a robot.

"All right."

Zacharie undid his shirt button by button. Jeremy could hardly swallow his saliva at the sight of this man undressing in front of him, who seemed to be taking his time in a lascivious way. His guest opened his shirt and removed it with difficulty, especially at the shoulders where it was tight due to the size of his arms. He revealed a powerful, well-shaped, hairy torso, just the way Jeremy liked it, as well as large, veiny biceps. The assistant felt his mouth go drier, especially when Zacharie took the shirt off entirely and tossed it to the floor, before standing up straight in front of him, as if awaiting further instructions.

The young man took his time to admire the man who was waiting, stiff as a post, his eyes on his. It was as if his gaze was asking: "And now that I'm shirtless, what do you want from me? Do you want me? To touch me? To caress my body? To enjoy every bit of it?"

Jeremy was in a conquering mood that he'd rarely experienced before. With a firmly-worded order, he had just undressed someone on command, and a stranger at that. He'd never done that before, and he never thought he'd ever have such confidence. He was thirsty for more. For this stranger to take it all off, jump on him and take him wildly on the sink. The thought alone made his crotch swell.

Neither of them had paid attention to the Iberian model who had quietly joined them in the bathroom. With Zacharie still, and his eyes fixed on Jeremy, the handsome stranger came slowly forward and gazed at them with envy. Nothing had escaped the Spaniard's notice, and it was now impossible for him to turn back. The sexual tension was palpable, and the temptation was through the roof. Jeremy studied him from top to bottom, a ferocious appetite in his eyes. More confident than he'd ever been in his life, he urged him to come closer with a nod. Something was rising inside him, electrifying every inch of his body. A mad, powerful, almost suppressed desire.

"You, come here and get shirtless too," he ordered.

The young model stared intently at him. His eyes froze, as if he were taking the time to understand the instruction he had received. After a slight hesitation, he moved towards Jeremy and Zacharie. All three stood in a tight space. Barely a few inches separated them. Inhabited by an overwhelming desire, they had no intention of leaving it at that. The silence was such that all that could be heard were their breaths, panting, just inches from each other's mouths.

The model lasciviously removed his jacket and tossed it to the floor in turn, before unbuttoning his shirt and ending up shirtless, revealing a slim, dry, hairless body. The three men studied each other, getting even closer. Their hands itched to touch, to discover each other. Their mouths began to open, breathless and excited. Deep down, Jeremy could hardly believe it. Two boys stood in front of him, seemingly waiting for his orders.

Listening only to the desire, Jeremy leaped passionately onto the thirty-something's mouth in a fiery French kiss. The stranger responded ardently, their tongues meeting frantically. Their hands discovered each other's bodies at last. The young

Iberian started caressing them, running from their backs to their bottoms.

Jeremy, like a love-starved man tormented by instinct, had no desire to choose between these two men who offered themselves to him without flinching. His mouth now tasted the model's, who didn't flinch and received him with pleasure. Their tongues mingled in a fury of passion, sometimes to the point of failing to breathe. Meanwhile, Zacharie took the opportunity to kiss the neck of the young assistant, who felt consumed by desire. Their hands became more pressing and exposing, moving from buttocks to crotch, eliciting ever more pronounced moans.

To hell with disturbing them! To hell with Maxime! Caroline was right.

Jeremy wanted to forget everything tonight and not have to choose. In the toilets of the Louvre, he couldn't have dreamed of a better way to "bounce back" and wanted to enjoy this heaven-sent chance to see his orders listened to and followed to the letter. All the while aware that they might be caught in the act at any moment.

It was his decision and nobody else's.

❧

Upstairs, the Vase of Varakk moved with slight jolts. The bronze stopper began to shift, gradually revealing a field of energy bubbling with fury inside the amphora as wishes were made.

❧

Zacharie, the Spaniard and Jeremy continued to burn with desire as if their lives depended on it. They moved from one to the other, kissing passionately and running their hands over each other enviously. Jeremy then ordered the thirty-year-old to remove his pants. He did it without hesitation, displaying a generous arousal that he struggled to keep discreet. It didn't take long for Jeremy to get down on his knees to honor him, while Zacharie played with the Iberian model's tongue, guiding the assistant's head.

A few delicious minutes later, Zacharie returned the favor, and Jeremy kissed the Spaniard, not to be outdone. Both united in their desire to satisfy the thirty-something's mouth. The antique dealer had mastered his technique, which was perfect, and knew how to excite and satisfy two partners at the same time.

Jeremy, still possessed and scarlet-eyed, seemed devoured by the intoxication of the moment. He ordered Zacharie to take care of the Iberian who, listening only to his desire, turned, pressing himself against the wall to offer his bottom. He received him, with difficulty at first, then with a pleasure he found hard to conceal. Jeremy, in turn, came to stand behind the thirty-year-old, who also welcomed him, with more guttural moans. He clutched at his solid shoulders and his taut stomach, slippery with perspiration, to the rhythm of his loins.

So much skin and sweat made Jeremy go wild with desire. His handsome guest and the Iberian model joined him in ecstasy. Staggering, trembling and clammy, the three of them silently caressed and kissed each other for long minutes until their excitement subsided.

❧

Each gradually emerged from his torpor as he withdrew from the other's mouth. They looked at each other, still red with sweat, and couldn't help but smile. On their faces, each seemed to say to the other, "Wow! What have we just done?" They stood back, wordlessly, in an almost embarrassed silence. They couldn't explain the impulse that had driven and inhabited them so powerfully. All three of them had wanted it, as if a force had driven them into each other's arms. They each picked up their belongings and got dressed in silence.

Getting dressed in a hurry, the Spanish man seemed almost ashamed to have succumbed to the temptation in this way, and hardly dared to look at Jeremy and Zacharie. Facing the bathroom mirrors, he tried to tidy himself up, but with his messy hair, rosy cheeks and shirt tucked into his pants, it was no easy task. He combed his hair again, and despite some flyaways, exited the bathroom with a simple, timid "Er... thank you," before slipping out as quickly as possible.

With Jeremy and the antique dealer now alone, they smiled at each other and finished dressing separately. Their outfits were creased and the champagne on Zacharie's shirt had started to fade.

"At least it has almost dried out by now," said Jeremy.

"Oh, yes," laughed the thirty-year-old.

He understood that the Louvre assistant

was trying to lighten the mood. Surrendering to purely sexual pleasure was easy; dealing with the 'aftermath' was something else entirely, and far more complicated.

"I don't think I've seen you here before," Jeremy continued, fastening his buttons.

"I... Er... I took an invitation from a friend who couldn't make it tonight," he replied hesitantly.

"And what's your name, if you don't mind me asking?"

"Zacharie. Zacharie Pellam. I..."

"Zacharie Pellam? The art expert? The antique dealer on Rue de Rivoli?"

"That's me," he replied, delighted to be known.

"Ah... Er... I'm sorry, I didn't know, I...," stammered the assistant, turning pale.

"What are you sorry for? For... this? What just happened?" asked a surprised Zacharie, as he refastened his jacket.

"Uh, yeah. If this gets out, I could get fired."

Zacharie smiled as he adjusted the final buttons. He approached Jeremy's ear and whispered in a soft voice, "I have absolutely no regrets. I won't say a word. And if I could do it again, I would."

His gaze locked with his. Jeremy felt an electric

shock run through his body. The strength he'd felt earlier was gone. But if Zacharie had offered to do it again, right now, just the two of them, he would have done it without a care in the world.

"What's your name?" asked the antique dealer.

"Jeremy Pilovsky. I work here. I'm Sir James Abernathy's assistant, who worked on the collection on display tonight."

"Pleased to meet you, Jeremy," he said with an amused wink, holding out his hand. Let's just say we met at that superb exhibition at the Louvre. And congratulations – it's a success!"

The young man shook his hand in return, smiling and flattered by the compliment, before the guest set off.

"Maybe I'll see you later," said Zacharie, walking away. "I've got a mission tonight!"

He didn't give Jeremy time to react and headed for the stairs in a hurry.

The Louvre employee smiled politely and spent several long seconds looking at himself in the mirror. Now alone in the bathroom, he thought back to what he had just experienced.

This had never happened to him before. In the wild. Like this. With strangers. And without a condom! He realized he might have made a mistake, he who had always been so cautious. But why had he given in to the temptation? Normally so restrained and thoughtful, he wondered how he could have let himself go like that. It was as if, for a moment, he'd been someone else. Even if, inwardly, what he'd experienced had given him mad pleasure.

Chapter 6
And everything is about to change

Midnight had just struck. The hour when the dead came out of their tombs to join the living on November 1st. It was also the hour when witches returned home after spending the day tormenting humans.

Walking back into the Oriental Arts room, Jeremy sensed a strange atmosphere. The lights seemed to have dimmed, no one was talking, the music was barely audible and the guests seemed to be in a state of suspended animation. Even Caroline was wandering around like a zombie. It was as if time had stood still.

"Caro! What's going on here?"

But she ignored him, as if he didn't exist.

"Hey, are you all right?" he asked as he approached her.

Her eyes glassy and empty, she paid no attention to her colleague and sank into the crowd in a trance.

He looked around and noticed that all the guests were in the same state as her. Something strange was going on, but Jeremy didn't know what. Fear began to grip him.

Until, in his field of vision, he saw the Varakk Vase.

The amphora was shaking, as if someone trapped inside was trying to get out. The bronze stopper of the enormous relic, which had shifted even more, was about to come off. As for the face of the djinn sculpted on the wall, it displayed dazzling white eyes. A source of energy began to escape from the container, crackling on the surface. The young assistant seemed to be the only one to see it.

"What the hell is going on here?" he wondered aloud.

Suddenly, the vase stopped moving. Jeremy watched the cork fall with a frightful crash that echoed throughout the room, startling him. The bronze had dropped to the floor, partially shattering the tiles under the intensity of the fall.

Light, bright light this time, burst forth from inside the amphora. More powerful, it evaporated into the air, quickly followed by a dense dark smoke that seemed heavy enough to rise into the air, and overflow from the vase. The more energy spread, the more the surrounding area plunged into an eerie gloom. The thick, black emanation moved like an entity of its own, growing in size and, once on the ground, seemed eager to devour space.

On the far side of the gala hall, Jeremy spotted a preoccupied Zacharie heading for a staircase leading down to one of the exhibition's basements, which was off-limits to the public. Glad to see that at least two of them had not succumbed to the massive petrification, and fearing that the dark smoke might reach his feet, he set off in pursuit.

"Wait! Zacharie! Where are you going?" he shouted, chasing after him.

But the thirty-year-old hadn't heard him. Jeremy set off down the stairs. Once at the bottom, the young man opened the only access door leading to a vast room, the same size as the gala room just above, where many of the museum's charms were normally stored. He almost bumped into his guest, who stood in the doorway amidst the Dantesque chaos.

A violent wind blew everything in its path: wood, papers, files. A terrible storm had broken out in this enclosed space. Jeremy couldn't believe his eyes. He and Zacharie could hardly stand under the power of the gust. The young assistant watched in awe as an enormous hole in the ground, made of some kind of energy material, exploded with lightning and fury. There was an immense bottomless pit, from which terrifying voices and heart-rending screams were also emerging, enough to frighten even the most reckless. The pit, with its demonic undertones, gradually grew in size and intensity. It was growing, slowly and visibly.

Jeremy saw Sir Abernathy at the end of the room, on the other side of the supernatural opening, sprawled on the floor and lifeless.

"Sir!" he shouted, trying to get closer to him

"Don't go! It's too late for him," cried Zacharie, grabbing him by the arm. "I couldn't stop all this in time, but nothing's lost yet."

"Stop what?" bellowed Jeremy, trying to make

himself heard over the surrounding noise.

"Varakk is back, and he's coming back to life! Sir Abernathy has been in his grip for too long and I suspected it. I knew it because of this..."

He showed him the talisman, the one that had shone in his Haussmann apartment in the Rue de Rivoli. It was a kind of medallion, barely larger than his palm, circular, pierced in the middle, with hieroglyphs engraved on it, as well as other ancient languages that Jeremy didn't immediately recognize.

"What is it?"

"It's an amulet that my family has held for generations. It's used to combat powerful demons from ancestral times and 'senses' coming dangers. It warned me of a threat around here last night. Cross-referencing all the information I had in my possession, something was whispering to me that I should come here tonight for the exhibition. And I wasn't wrong!"

"But... your thing doesn't make sense!"

"And yet, look!" he said, pointing to the otherworldly mouth on the ground, gaping even wider, as the demonic storm blew harder.

"What happened?" Jeremy shouted again to make himself heard.

"I have no idea. It seems that the seal on the Vase of Varakk has been broken. My guess is that he used the wishes of your guests to assert his power. The same thing happened thousands of years ago. And tonight, everyone took part in his resurrection.

Jeremy swallowed. He thought back to the wish he'd made. And that would have led to...? No, it couldn't be true!

"Let's go back up! I haven't said my last word," shouted Zacharie, sure of himself.

"We can't leave Sir Abernathy on the ground!"

"It's not too late to save him, but there's nothing we can do for him now. Come with me, or we'll all be swallowed up!"

The opening to the Other World was still growing. Both ran up the stairs and found themselves back in the exhibition room, now bathed in darkness, barely lit by the moon.

Chapter 7
Varakk

Jeremy and Zacharie stood at the edge of the stairs, at the entrance to the gala room. The sight stunned them. All the guests were lying on the floor in a deep sleep. A tide of men and women. The stillness was mournful, in an atmosphere almost devoid of light. Jeremy swallowed his saliva and whispered, trying to zigzag between the people:

"What the hell?"

"They've been bewitched..." breathed Zacharie, who was following him.

"Aren't they dead?"

"No. At least, I don't think so. If you look closely,

you can see their rib cages moving."

Jeremy scanned the bodies of a few of the guests and realized, partly reassured, that Zacharie was right.

"But why weren't we hit, too?" resumed the young assistant.

"Maybe because we were 'busy' downstairs during the attack…"

"From the attack? But from who?" cut in Jeremy, his cheeks turning pink.

He had no time to listen to Zacharie's reply. The black smoke rising from the amphora redoubled its power and exploded into the air until it flattened out. Zacharie and Jeremy, startled, fell silent and squinted to get a better look. The emanation gradually gave way to a form. Someone was sitting on the vase, one foot dangling, the other bent. The appearance became clearer as the silence grew more deafening.

It was a man. His eyes closed, he seemed to be thinking. Zacharie and Jeremy gasped and tried not to make a sound. Something both frightening and supernatural was unfolding before them.

❧

The stranger in the vase opened his sublime violet eyes, shining in the half-light and highlighted by the kohl applied to his eyelids. Dressed in a dark-toned royal sarouel, he was bare-chested, displaying a voluminous body with chiseled muscles set off by caramel skin. His beautiful short curly black hair accentuated his fine, elegant face.

Varakk held their gaze.

"Who's there?" he asked in a suave, cavernous voice, as he straightened up gracefully.

He levitated, before gently setting foot on the ground.

There was something noble in his gait, slow and controlled, with an incandescent charm. He stopped a few yards from Zacharie and Jeremy, who hadn't moved. His body was more impressive up close. Very tall, with a perfect arrogant stance, his shoulders were broad, his biceps bulging and his robust torso, hairless and dry, hid none of his innumerable bulging muscles. Even in the dark, his power shone through.

"I recognize the mark of the Pellams," he breathed thoughtfully, looking at Zacharie. "Your family's been giving me a hard time for thousands of years. And you... who are you?"

Jeremy was afraid. The djinn was watching him with an unnerving insistence.

"It doesn't matter, Varakk!" said Zacharie, suddenly pouncing on him.

With a snap of his fingers, the demon sent him hurtling through the air. The thirty-something flew across the gala room before colliding hard with a wall and falling heavily to the floor. The frightened young assistant shrieked in surprise, horrified by the supernatural vividness of the attack. Such was the violence of the impact, Zacharie didn't get up immediately.

The rapid offensive sent Jeremy into a tizzy of terror. Panicked, he thought he was living through a waking nightmare. He could hardly breathe and his heart was beating so fast that his chest felt like it was going to explode. Varakk looked at him again, taking the time to study him from top to bottom. When he gracefully stepped towards him, the young assistant realized that he could no longer move, as if held back by a magnetic force.

"You're the one who wanted to have more confidence in yourself, aren't you?"

Jeremy yelped. He couldn't believe what was happening to him. Varakk moved even closer and placed his face close to his, their chests almost touching. The djinn seemed to take particular pleasure in making him uncomfortable.

"«Did you get what you were looking for?" he asked him in a soft voice, coming closer, as if he were about to kiss him.

Jeremy didn't move. He couldn't. His heart was pounding. Varakk smiled and began to circle the young man with controlled steps, grinning from ear to ear as he gracefully stroked his chin and then one cheek with his fingertip.

"Have I answered your wish?" the djinn asked again.

The demon, now behind him, slid his hand up and down Jeremy's back in a carnal manner. Then he brought his face close to Jeremy's ear

"I think so, because I can feel it," Varakk whispered in a sensual voice. You enjoyed it and you liked it."

The Louvre employee shuddered. His doubts had been dispelled. What had happened earlier in the bathroom was the work of the djinn, the result of his wish! But like the Cartesian he was, he refused to accept this explanation. It couldn't be possible! Wishes didn't exist, he mused.

"Oh, yes, they exist. I'm real. And all of you here are mine now," concluded the demon, moving back to face him.

Varakk also possessed the power of mind reading! He continued to look at Jeremy, this time from further away. The djinn wore an envious pout, as if he regarded the Louvre employee as his future dessert. Jeremy shrieked.

For his part, Zacharie, still a little stunned, got to his feet.

"Varakk. You won't get away with this. I... I..."

"What are you up to, Pellam's son?" the demon snapped, turning around in annoyance.

The energy field activated on Jeremy dissipated and the young assistant was finally able to move his limbs.

"What are you going to do to me? I've got the freedom I deserve!" declared Varakk solemnly, his big arms open wide. I see that humans haven't changed in all this time..."

"You don't deserve anything, Varakk! I remind you that you've been locked up for making a pact with the dark forces!" shouted Zacharie, limping towards him.

"I'm doing what I exist to do on Earth: granting

wishes…" he replied calmly.

"It's not true! You want to plunge the world into the underworld to gain power. But that won't happen!"

Zacharie raised his talisman to the sky and shouted an incantation in a language Jeremy didn't recognize. Varakk's gaze changed. His face, hitherto seemingly gentle, metamorphosed and became more evil, revealing sharp canines.

Zacharie's amulet glowed with a dazzling light. An electrical energy surged. It was such that it exploded in a wave of force that swept through the exhibition hall and its surroundings. Blinded, the djinn stepped back.

❧

Deep in Mesopotamia, in the middle of a stony desert, from a thousand-year-old cavern dug into the rock that no one knew existed anymore, the ground shook. Slowly at first, then the seismic waves amplified.

Suddenly, a powerful beam of light exploded from the earth and pointed skywards, ripping through the darkness of the black night The energy source, which came from deep within the Earth, changed direction once it reached the atmosphere, heading straight for the Louvre.

❧

Varakk opened his eyes again. The Oriental Arts room was immersed in a strange atmosphere, illuminated by a hazy gray light emanating from the amulet still in Zacharie's hand. Time seemed to have stood still.

"Are you going to fight me, Pellam's son? It's too late!" screamed the demon. "The mouth of the Netherworld is open and it's going to swallow up this place and all those damned people who made their wishes to me! I'm more powerful than ever and ready to claim my revenge!"

A dazzling diaphanous light fell on the Louvre from the sky, blinding those in the museum, with everyone shielding their eyes. Until it disappeared, as quickly as it had appeared. White dots dazzled Varakk, Jeremy and Zacharie as they recovered their sight.

❧

A hoarse, terrifying, monstrous sound echoed around them. The ground shook with heavy footsteps for meters around. The sound of a dark animal scream approached. The djinn's face grew doubtful. He turned back to Zacharie, whose amulet continued to glow.

"You dared to call him? Because you think he's going to get me again?"

He was unable to finish his diatribe. One of the walls of the exhibition hall exploded in a monumental crash of rubble and dust that took them all by surprise. Jeremy screamed and covered his face from the falling debris. Zacharie still hadn't moved from his side.

Bahamut, the legendary dragon of ancient times, appeared before them, furious. Titanic, some ten meters tall, he could hardly spread his wings in this interior space, which he had just partly destroyed. His skin resembled that of crocodiles, and spikes adorned parts of his body. Irritated, he seemed impatient to do battle once his attention was focused on Varakk. His eyes glowed red and his throat held back from spitting out his rage as he recognized his age-old enemy.

Above his head, a proud, handsome rider with oriental features looked down at Varakk, who was now levitating in the air in front of him.

"Bolaam! Wherever I am, you'll always be there!" snarled the genie.

He too had spotted his most loyal nemesis, the one he'd battled with for far too many years before. Bolaam, the legendary djinn, dressed in a gold and blue tunic, a gigantic sword at his waist and a voluminous turban that matched the harmonious attributes of his tanned face.

"I remind you that our fates are linked," replied Bolaam. "I've locked you up before, and I'll do it again as often as necessary."

No sooner had he finished his sentence than the colossal winged creature leaped at the djinn before landing heavily on the ground, knocking over numerous artifacts and causing inestimable damage in its path. Spitting fire, the legendary beast rampaged through the exhibition hall, which was far too small for him, but he seemed determined to make mincemeat of Varakk.

"Do you need your Bahamut?" Varakk shouted at him as he levitated.

Flying at breakneck speed to escape his attackers, he held his ground against the dragon.

"Bolaam! Just try to beat me! I've got a score to settle with you!" Varakk challenged.

*

At the same moment, Zacharie unfurled his amulet again and shouted another incantation. Dark and mournful, his voice echoed throughout the Louvre, amplified tenfold by the talisman's power. As the battle between the two djinns and the dragon intensified and spilled outside into the courtyard of the Louvre, not far from the pyramid, the ground began to tremble once again.

Several artifacts in the museum glowed. With his incantation complete, Zacharie tucked his amulet away in his pocket and rushed over to Jeremy, taking him by the arm.

"Take cover! It's not going to be pretty," he shouted.

Not far from them, outside, Bahamut was fighting, guided by Bolaam, against Varakk, who was hurling demonic blue fire with his own hands. Although they were fighting as a pair, the evil genius was dominating the battle, galvanized by this evening of wishes, and was determined to emerge victorious.

Hiding behind one of the gala's ephemeral bars, Jeremy and Zacharie suddenly heard cries of fury approaching them, like a ferocious army about to disembark. With a din of thunder, several doors of the exhibition hall were smashed open, startling Jeremy with simultaneous blasts of explosions. He tried to look around, but couldn't believe what he was witnessing.

Painted figures, statues, sculptures and other artifacts known to the Louvre poured into the room, before his bewildered eyes. Works of art from the museum were coming to life before his very eyes! Emperor Augustus, Marcus Aurelius, Marie de' Medici, Ariadne, Hadrian, Alexander the Great and even Liberty, from Delacroix's painting, entered furiously to help Bolaam. Out of their paintings and their safety cabinets, they had abandoned their decor to join the defender of the Earth. Zacharie had just called on the souls embodied in the most important works of art in the Louvre to help defeat Varakk.

A Dantesque battle ensued against this army

of the arts. Now alone against the all-comers, the genius began to find it difficult to use his powers against such a troop of spirits determined not to be dictated to.

Emperor Augustus, aided by Marcus Aurelius, threw himself at him with his sword. Alexander the Great, riding Bucephalus, tried to catch him in the air. Marie de' Medici, meanwhile, watched the battle from a corner, drinking her tea. She had no aptitude for battle and intended to confine herself to what she had always done in the past: watch her fellow men fight for her and let Liberty guide them, all of them.

Jeremy didn't recognize everyone who had been called in as reinforcements. Several figures, even minor ones from the Louvre's greatest paintings, drew their swords, bows and guns. Varakk continued to flit through the air, avoiding several attacks and fending off others. Despite the power of the hell mouth he had opened, he was beginning to tire and seemed to lack the evil power to take the fight to so many magical beings.

The battle, impressive as it was, didn't last long. Driven back into the gala hall, and cornered on all sides amid the surrounding ruins, Varakk found himself trapped with his back to his own vase. The museum spirits, who had gathered in front of him to prevent him from escaping, gave way to Bolaam's legendary dragon, who approached him, looking as furious as ever.

Faced with the terrified djinn, the Bahamut opened its impressive jaws, revealing many sharp teeth with which to bite him. But Varakk didn't have the courage to face death. Frightened, he jumped back into his vase, which was immediately closed by Bolaam. The latter, endowed with phenomenal power, replaced the bronze stopper with the titanic strength of his arms. Using a beam from his eyes, he fused the joints to seal the amphora once again, as he had done a millennia before.

❧

Calm returned to the great hall, which had been destroyed. Jeremy, stunned by what he had just seen, was equally astonished by the immeasurable damage he could only observe. Apart from the Varakk Vase, nothing in the exhibition was left intact, and the Louvre had been partly demolished. Not even the glass pyramid had withstood Bahamut's onslaught!

He didn't know what to feel; it had all been so fast and... unreal! Had that fight even been real? Had he dreamed it all? He pinched himself. No, he hadn't been dreaming.

Opposite him, every art spirit from the Louvre who had taken part in the confrontation rose into the sky and vanished one by one into a cloud of white light. The many 'collaborators' quietly left the battlefield to return to their artifacts, sculptures and paintings.

Zacharie rose to join Bolaam and, in relative calm, held up his amulet to activate it once more.

"Thank you for helping me," he breathed, as the legendary dragon, who had returned outside, began to disappear, but not before offering a curtsy to the antique dealer.

"You have done well, Zacharie Pellam. I owe your lineage eternal gratitude, and I've always kept my word."

"It's not too hard there, in your dimension?"

The genie, about to leave this world, was amused by the question.

"Let's just say I'm given interesting missions. It's better than dying forever. I think you know something about that... Goodbye, Zacharie."

"Goodbye, Bolaam," he replied, with a respectful smile.

The dragon vanished in turn, along with its owner rider.

Zacharie's amulet continued to glow. With the spirits now all back in their places in the Louvre, the much-destroyed Oriental Arts room was put back together before Jeremy's astonished eyes. In front of him, the walls were rebuilt, the pieces of the exhibition that had been destroyed were reformed and everything was restored in just a few seconds, in an aerial waltz of objects and materials. The pale gray glow that had illuminated the room throughout the battle gradually disappeared as Zacharie's talisman was extinguished for good. The electricity came back on, the music started up again, and those asleep on the floor gradually woke up and sat up gently. The strange, demonic light that had dominated their gaze faded. Gradually, the guests resumed their festivities as if nothing had happened. Some even wondered why the contents of their glasses were empty, or even spilled on the floor.

Sir James Abernathy, looking stunned, appeared in the room and observed the crowd present at his show. He seemed relieved that the evening was going so well. Caroline, accompanied by Nathalie, finally found him and told him that some generous future patrons wanted to see him. This Halloween event would mark a turning point in the art world, he was now convinced.

Chapter 8
As if nothing had happened

"How? By what miracle? How is this possible?" asked Jeremy of Zacharie.

"That's the strength of this amulet," he replied. "It's very... special, you might say. It can protect a battlefield if used in time. And thus erase all traces of magic. It's been very useful in the past. To my ancestors and to me."

"But I... I don't understand what just happened," Jeremy continued, lost. "I'm in a dream, aren't I?"

Zacharie smiled.

"It's normal to feel that way. And no, it wasn't a dream. At the same time, you're not supposed to witness this kind of event... I'm a little embarrassed because I'm going to have to erase your memory."

Jeremy shivered. Zacharie had addressed him with a rather bored expression. He wondered how he would do it.

"Don't erase the whole evening..." Jeremy tried, his cheeks flushed, emphasizing the word "whole."

Zacharie took a few seconds to understand what Jeremy meant. Then he smiled. Before he could open his mouth again, the young assistant spoke first.

"Are you really an antiques dealer?"

"Let's just say I'm a recognized art expert. That's my official description. But it's a front, as I'm sure you've gathered by now."

"I'd like to know more," said Jeremy, genuinely interested.

Zacharie wasn't fooled. He suspected Jeremy was stalling for time. He would have to wait before erasing his memory.

"Wow... It's a long story. Given what happened between the three of us earlier in the bathroom and your use of the djinn's power on me, you already know a lot of intimate things about me," he replied with a wink.

Jeremy's face turned peony red. Something

insane had indeed happened earlier, it was true.

"I... I don't know what to say..." he stammered.

Zacharie smiled to see him so embarrassed.

"Come on, even though we were in his thrall, we still wanted to... And I found it rather fun, I must admit," he reassured him with another wink.

Jeremy felt his mobile vibrate. A message, which he was quick to consult.

WhatsApp. From: Maxime.

We barely had a chance to talk earlier. I wanted to tell you that I didn't want to be a source of negativity for you... I know you care about me. Will you forgive me?

He read the message several times, almost dazed, in retrospect, by his ex-lover's nerve. He felt like shouting a monumental "assssshoooooole!" But since he wasn't alone, and he was at a chic party full of 'beautiful people,' he preferred to press the best button there is: 'Block contact.'

He closed his smartphone, took a deep breath and watched the mundane event unfold before his eyes, still in shock from the last three completely unreal hours. He felt his head about to explode. Ten thousand questions were racing through it, and he wanted to ask them all to his handsome savior from the Louvre. He turned to him.

"Since we already know each other... intimately, and haven't done things in the right order, Sir, would you care to join me for a drink at Café Marly, right next door, just the two of us?"

"I think we can drop the formality now, don't you, Jeremy? And I'd be delighted," replied Zacharie, a smile cracking on his lips.

He'd erase his memory later. Maybe.

Madelline R. Kennedy

Madelline, a shy 33-year-old American and avid Francophile from San Diego, who has been living in Normandy for several years with her French husband, loves Jérôme's world, and wanted to join him in the adventure of writing.

Jérôme Patalano

A Parisian advertising executive, 45-year-old Jérôme was nurtured by the French iconic TV show "Club Dorothée" *(1988-1997 - which imported manga culture to France, contributing, 20 years later, to making France the world's leading consumer of manga after Japan)* and the American movies made in the '80s and '90s. He loves to spend his time losing himself in his fertile imagination, especially during very boring meetings. He is the proud author of several fantasies and urban fantasy novels published *(in France: Alter Real Editions, Inceptio Editions & le Cherche Midi)* and self-published.

If you liked the story, please feel free to tell us about it on Amazon, Goodreads and on your social networks.

From Jérôme Patalano

2024 – Amazon KDP: 3h01 - Petites histoires fantastiques et horrifiques entre nous *(courtes histoires d'horreur - participant aux Plumes francophones 2024).*

2023 – Amazon KDP: Zacharie & Jérémie Rencontre surnaturelle au Louvre.

2022 — Inceptio Éditions: *De l'autre côté des étoiles* (YA fantastique) - ***Book no longer available, but will soon be available again as a self-publication!***

2021 — Vivlio Studio App: *Une nuit de 1948* (policier).

2021 — YouTube, podcast en 3 épisodes: « L'Amour en Provence », pour la marque L'Occitane (romance).

2020 — Alter Real Éditions: *Magical London* (urban fantasy) — réédité en 2022 sous le nom de *Knocking on Hell's Door.*

2019 — Cherche Midi: « 2 184 », dans le recueil *Musiques de parfums* (science-fiction dystopique).

How to contact Jérôme & Madelline :

Website: jeromepatalano.fr

Facebook: Jérôme Patalano - Auteur

Instagram & Threads: @jerome_patalano_auteur

Legal registration: October 2024
ISBN: 978-2-9589893-3-0

www.ingramcontent.com/pod-product-compliance
Lightning Source LLC
LaVergne TN
LVHW090051160826
845672LV00015B/1642